chronicle books · san francisco

Duck! Rabbit!

AMY KROUSE ROSENTHAL & TOM LICHTENHELD

Hey, look! A duck!

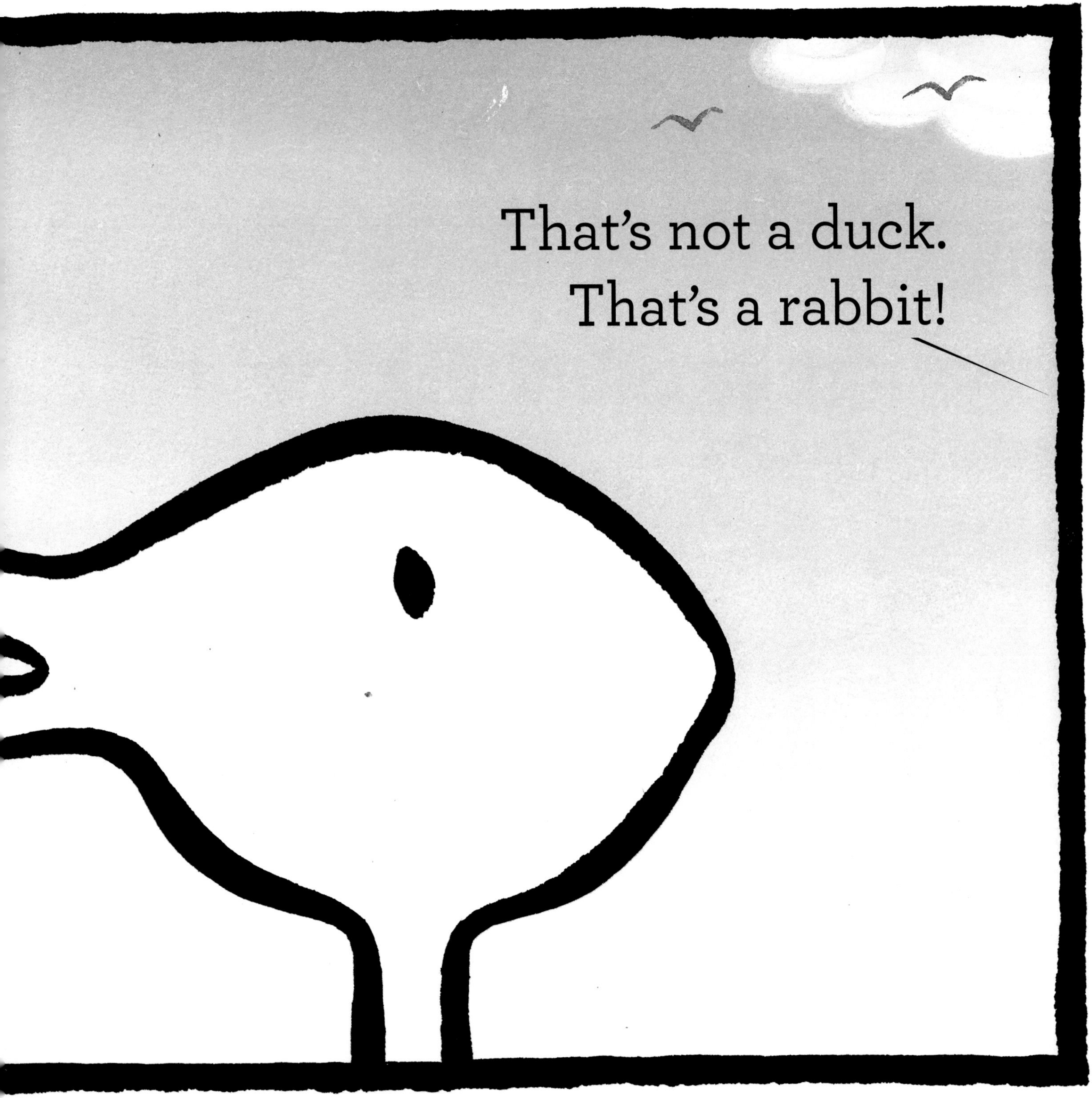
That's not a duck.
That's a rabbit!

Are you kidding me?
It's totally a duck.

See, there's his bill.

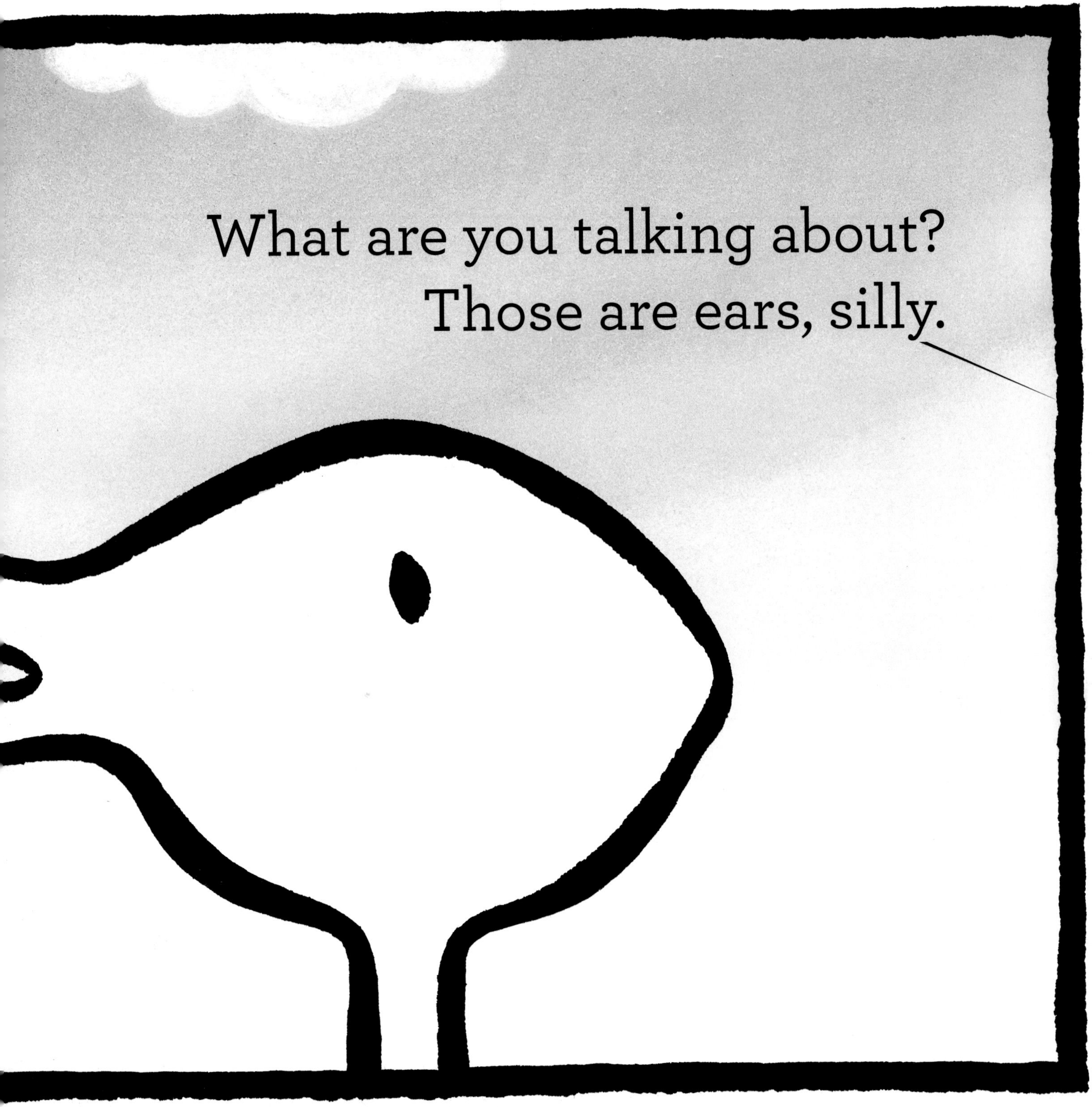
What are you talking about?
Those are ears, silly.

It's a duck. And he's about to eat a piece of bread.

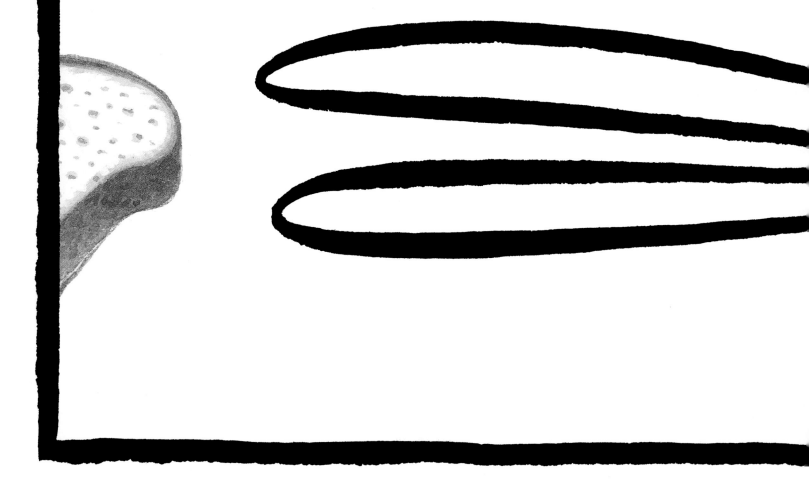

It's a rabbit. And he's about to eat a carrot.

Wait. Listen. Did you hear that?
I heard duck sounds.

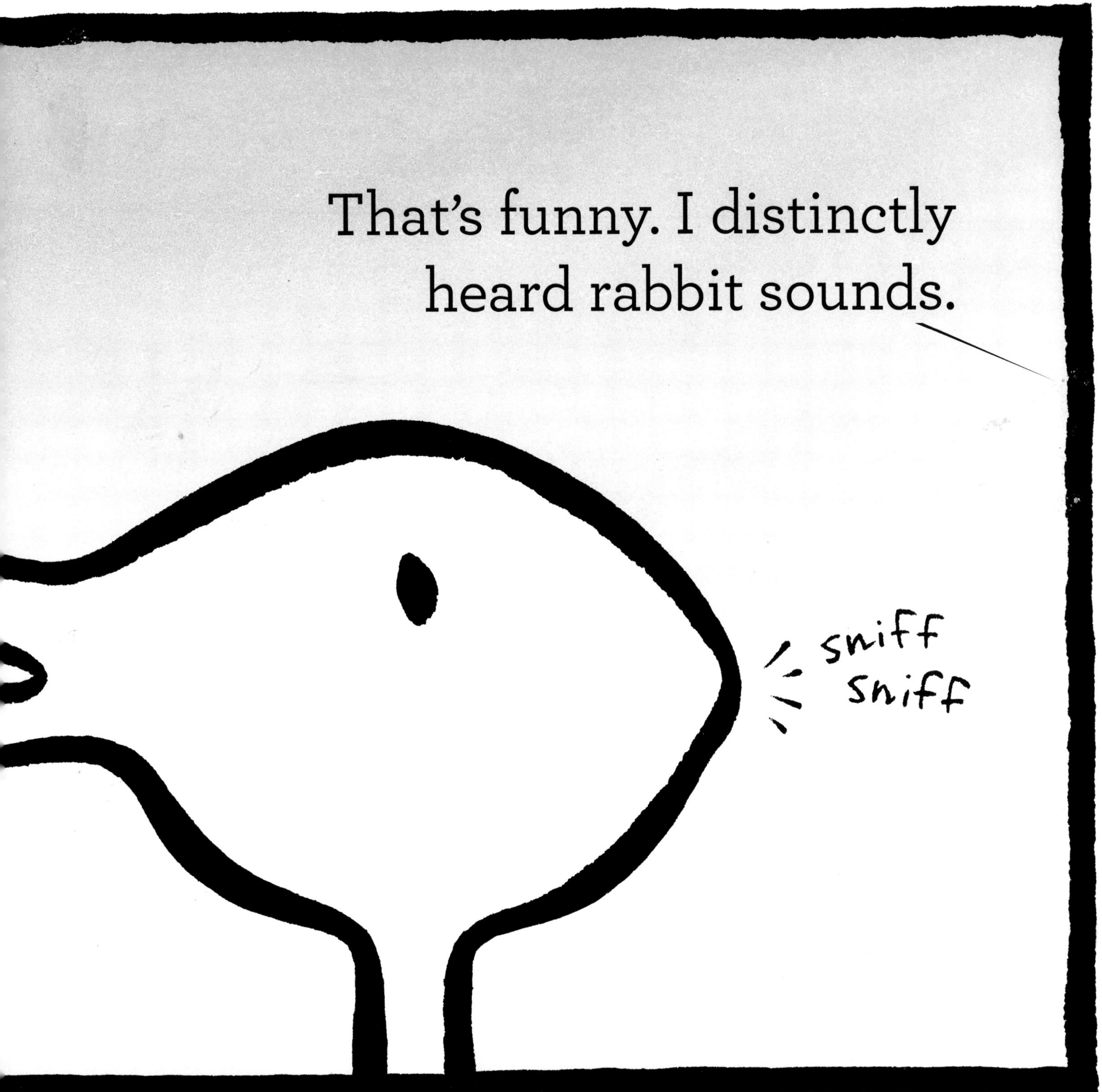
That's funny. I distinctly heard rabbit sounds.
sniff sniff

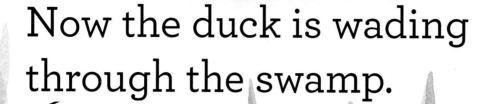

Now the duck is wading through the swamp.

No, the rabbit is hiding in the grass.

There, see? It's flying!

Here,
look at
the duck
through my
binoculars.

Sorry,
still a
rabbit.

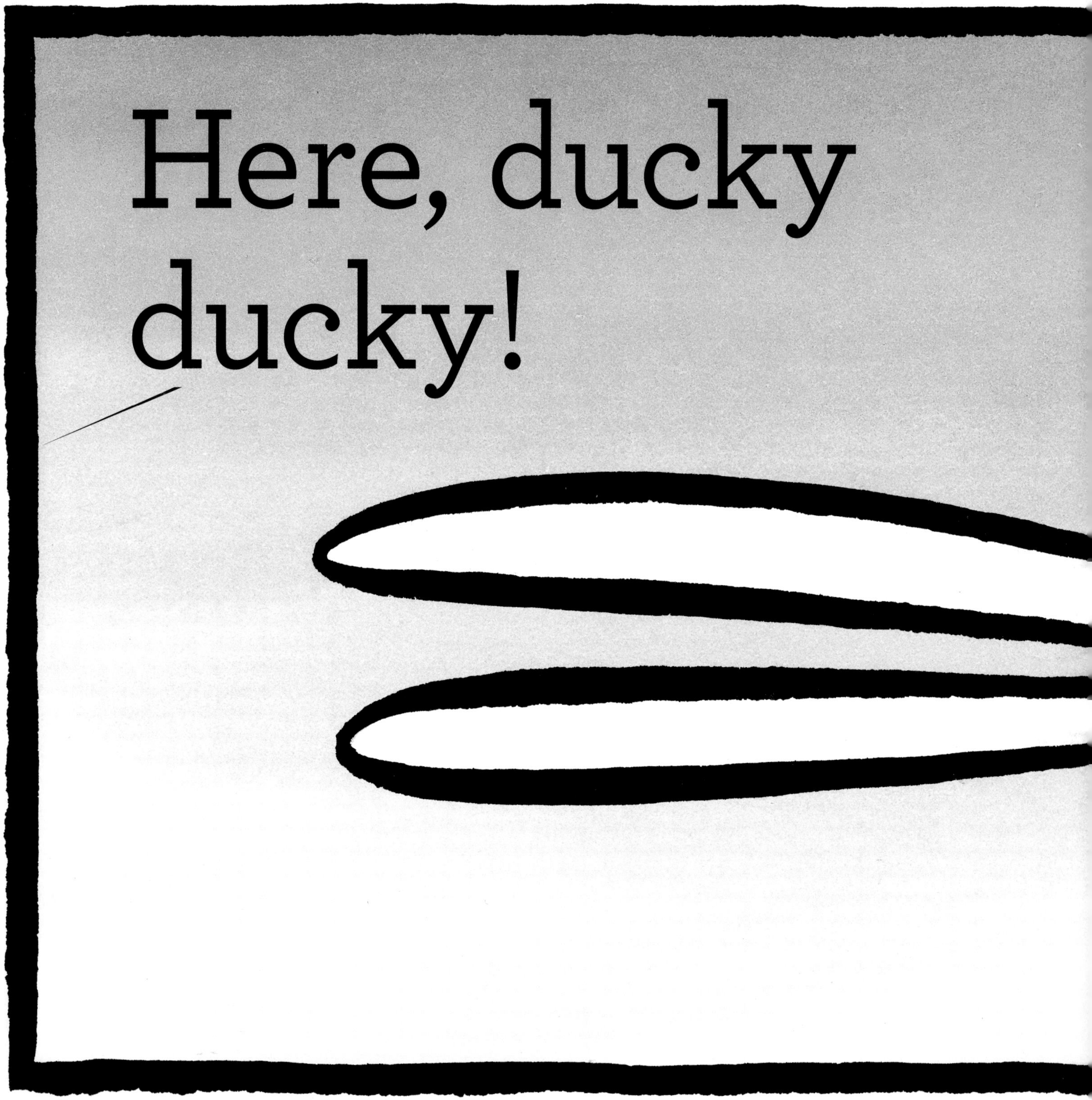
Here, ducky ducky!

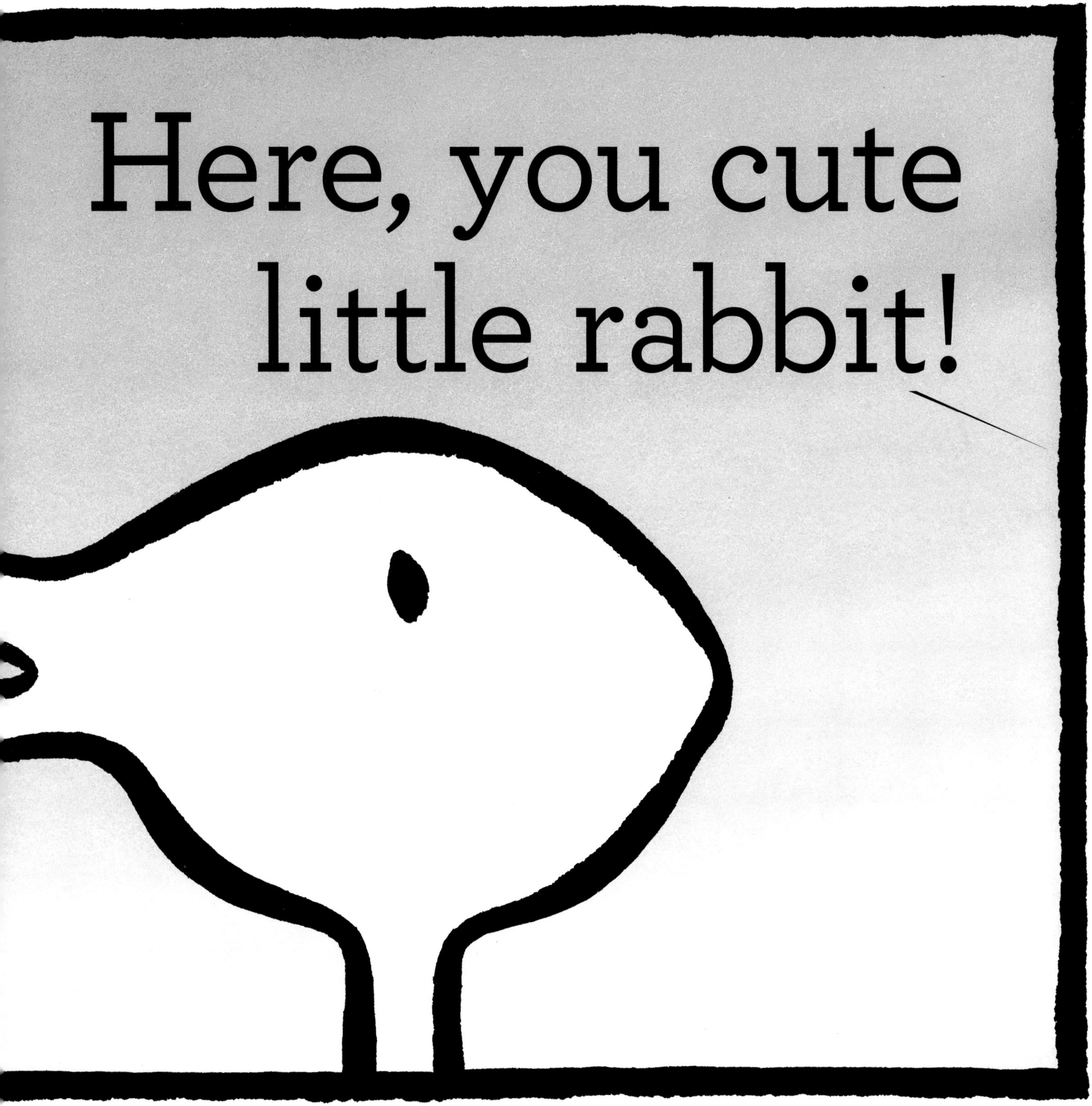
Here, you cute little rabbit!

Oh great, you scared him away.

I didn't scare him away.
You scared him away.

You know, maybe you were right.
Maybe it *was* a rabbit.

Thing is, now I'm actually thinking it was a duck.

Well, anyway...now what
do you want to do?

I don't know. What do *you* want to do?

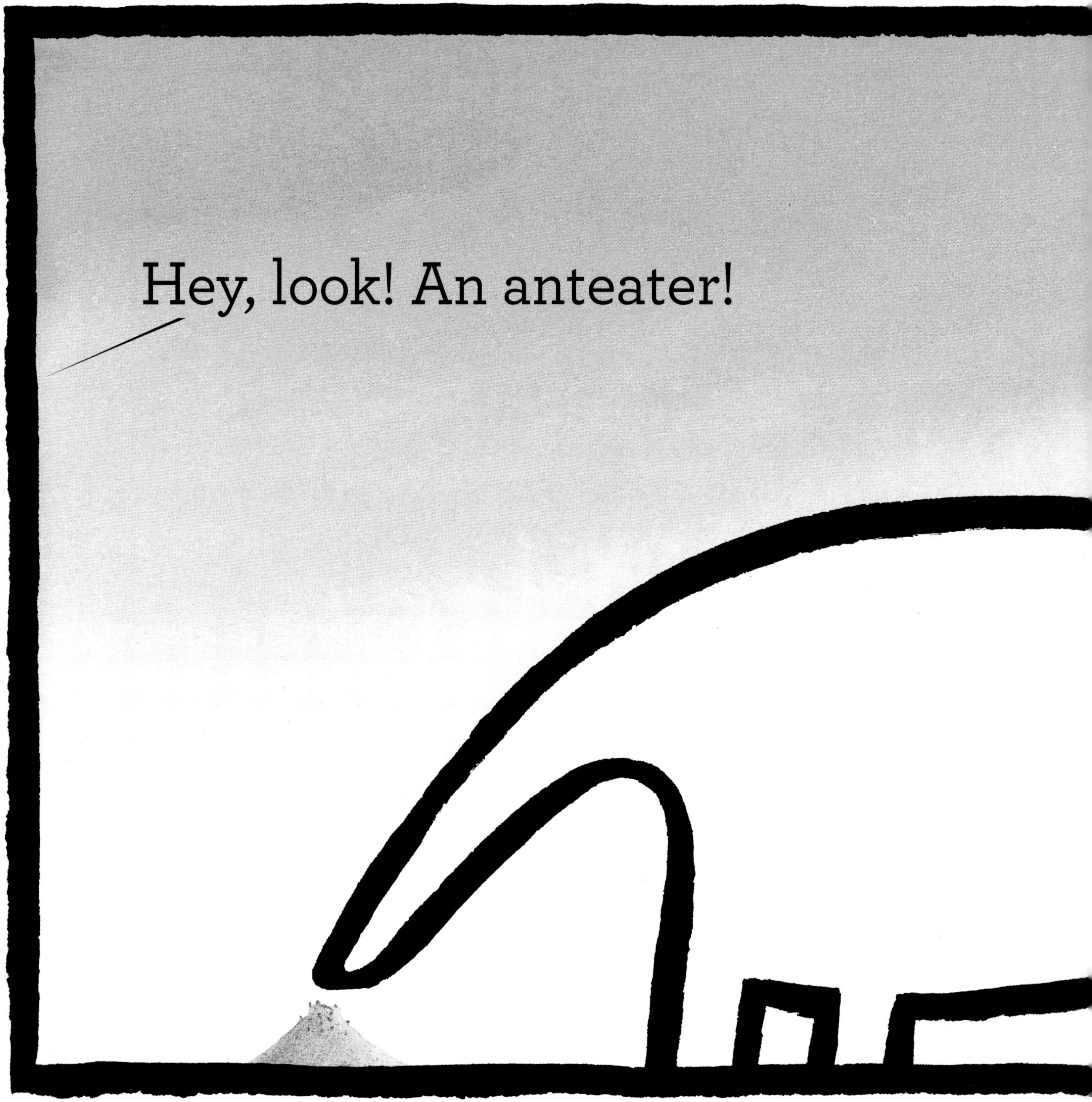
Hey, look! An anteater!

That's no anteater.
That's a brachiosaurus!

The End.

(It's not the end! There's still all this stuff!)

Thanks to Jan for her unwavering support.
Thanks to Eric Rohmann and Larry Day for their artful camaraderie. —T. L.

Duck . . . duck . . . duck . . . GOOSE! I pick Charise Mericle Harper. —A. K. R.

And thanks to Marshall Ross for putting us in the same room. —T. L. and A. K. R.

Text © 2009 by Amy Krouse Rosenthal.
Illustrations © 2009 by Tom Lichtenheld.
All rights reserved.
No part of this book may be reproduced in any form
without written permission from the publisher.

Book design by Tom Lichtenheld and Kristine Brogno.
Typeset in Archer.
The illustrations were rendered in ink, watercolor, and a wee bit of colored pencil.
Manufactured by Toppan Leefung Da Ling Shan Town, Dongguan, China, in May 2010.

Library of Congress Cataloging-in-Publication Data
Rosenthal, Amy Krouse.
Duck! Rabbit! / [text by] Amy Krouse Rosenthal ; [illustrations by] Tom Lichtenheld.
p. cm.
Summary: Two unseen characters argue about whether
the creature they are looking at is a rabbit or a duck.
ISBN 978-0-8118-6865-5
[1. Animals—Identification—Fiction.] I. Lichtenheld, Tom, ill. II. Title.
PZ7.R719445Duc 2009
[E]—dc22
2008028102

10 9 8 7 6 5 4

This product conforms to CPSIA 2008.

Chronicle Books LLC
680 Second Street, San Francisco, California 94107

www.chroniclekids.com